♡ Eva's Campfire Adventure ♡

Read more OWL DIARIES books!

OWL DIARIES

♥ Eva's Campfire Adventure ♥

Rebecca Elliott

BRANCHES™

SCHOLASTIC INC.

For our fabulous camping buddies
the Cheeseman family. xxx —R.E.

Library of Congress Cataloging-in-Publication Data

Names: Elliott, Rebecca, author. | Elliott, Rebecca. Owl Diaries.
Title: Eva's Campfire Adventure / Rebecca Elliott.
Description: First edition. | New York : Scholastic, Inc., 2020. | Series:
Owl diaries | Summary: Eva Wingdale and her owl classmates are on a
camping trip to the other side of the forest, where one of the
assignments is to make useful inventions—but Eva and Lucy become
totally distracted by the legend of Nellie Wingdale, founder of
Treetopolis and her buried treasure, and never finish their project.
Identifiers: LCCN 2019020999 | ISBN 9781338298697 (paperback) | ISBN
9781338298710 (reinforced library binding)
Subjects: LCSH: Owls—Juvenile fiction. | Camping—Juvenile fiction. |
Treasure troves—Juvenile fiction. | Diaries—Juvenile fiction. | CYAC:
Owls—Fiction. | Camping—Fiction. | Buried treasure—Fiction. | Diaries—Fiction.

Classification: LCC PZ7.E45812 Eug 2020 | DDC [Fic]--dc23

LC record available at https://lccn.loc.gov/2019020999

Classification: LCC PZ7.E45812 Tr 2019 | DDC [Fic]—dc23 LC record available
at https://lccn.loc.gov/2018053289

10 9 8 7 6 5 4 3 2 1   20 21 22 23 24

Printed in China   62
First edition, January 2020

Edited by Katie Carella
Book design by Maria Mercado

♡ Table of Contents ♡

1 Let's Go Camping!   1
2 Campfire Fun   12
3 An OWLMAZING Discovery   20
4 Follow the Clues!   30
5 Let's All Pulley Together!   48
6 Find That Treasure!   58

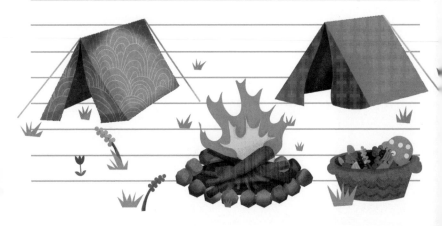

11

Woodpine Avenue

♡ Let's Go Camping! ♡

Sunday

Hi Diary,
 Guess **HOO**! It's your favorite owl –
Eva Wingdale!

 This week I'm going CAMPING!

<u>I love</u>:

The sound of
rain on a tent

Candy

Nature watching

The word <u>backpack</u>

Packing for a trip

 Solving problems

Playing outside

 Sitting around a campfire

<u>I DO NOT love:</u>

Rain leaking
through a tent

Candy sticking
to my feathers

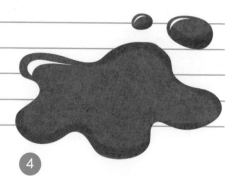

Being stuck
indoors

The word <u>mud</u>

 Forgetting to pack something important

 Impossible problems

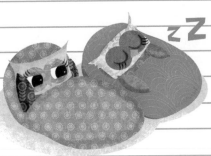 When friends snore

Mom's slug butter and jam sandwiches

This is my **OWLMAZING** family.

Dad

Mom

Humphrey

Baby Mo

Me

This is my pet bat, Baxter. He's such a cutie-pie.

I love being an owl!

We fly
almost silently.

We sleep in
the daytime.

Most owls **HOOT**, but some screech and some whinny like a horse!

HOOT!

SCREECH!

WHINNY

We love snuggling up together.

I live at number 11 Woodpine Avenue in Treetopolis.

My bestie, Lucy Beakman, lives next door.

My friends and I go to Treetop Owlementary. Here is our class photo:

Zac
Macy
Jacob
Zara
Kiera
Lucy
Sue
Lilly
Me
George
Hailey
Carlos
Mrs. Featherbottom

My class is going on a camping trip! I'm all packed.

Now I must go to sleep – so tomorrow comes quicker!

♡ Campfire Fun ♡

Monday

Mrs. Featherbottom led the way to the campsite.

Come on, class! The sooner we get there, the sooner we can have fun!

We weren't used to carrying such heavy backpacks, so we kept flying too close to the ground.

But we helped one another and got there in the end!

When we arrived, we got right to work.

George, Zara, Kiera, and Lilly set up the tents.

We will feel so cozy sleeping in these!

Carlos, Macy, and Sue gathered food for our dinner.

Hailey and Zac collected water from the river.

Lucy, Jacob, and I gathered logs to build a fire.

I LOVE camping!

Me too!

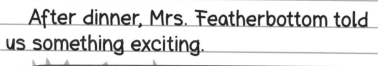

After dinner, Mrs. Featherbottom told us something exciting.

This week you have a project to complete. You'll work in pairs to build something <u>useful</u> out of materials you find in the forest.

Fun!

Will there be a prize for the best invention?

Yes! There will be a special trophy for the winners.

Ooooh!

We picked our partners.

I want that trophy! George, you're good at making things. You can be my partner.

Oh, okay.

Lucy and I chose to work together. We had NO idea what to make, but we knew we'd come up with something OWLMAZING!

Then we sat around the campfire toasting s'mores. YUM!

We **HOOTED** campfire songs.

We even sang a <u>special</u> version of my favorite song!

There was an owl who had a bat, and BAXTER was his name-o.
B–A–X–T–E-R
B–A–X–T–E-R
B–A–X–T–E-R
And Baxter was his name-o!

As the sun came up, we climbed into our sleeping bags. Our tents are so cozy! I don't think it will be long before we fall aslee . . . Zzzzzz.

3

♡ An OWLMAZING Discovery ♡

Tuesday

Tonight we woke up super-excited to start our forest projects.

Carlos and Zara searched for special feathers to make quill pens.

Sue and George looked for logs to make a catapult.

Hailey and Zac
gathered pine needles
to weave baskets.

Lilly and Jacob
collected willow to
make a hammock.

Macy and Kiera
searched for sticks
to hollow out to
make flutes.

Everyone had
great ideas. But
Lucy and I had
NO IDEAS!

Mrs. Featherbottom said we should all take a break and swim in the lake. It was such **FEATHER-SPLASHING** fun!

Then she told us a story: The Legend of Treetopolis. It was about Nellie Wingdale, the founder of Treetopolis.

Nellie Wingdale

Everyone went back to working on their projects.

But Lucy and I <u>still</u> didn't know what to make.

Lucy pulled a reed from my feathers.

Then she had a **WING-CREDIBLE** idea!

I had heard Hailey say there were lots of reeds by the river, so we went there to search. But when we got there, we found MUCH more than reeds!

Lucy! Do you see those old pebbles? It looks like they're in the shape of a letter!

Not a letter, Eva. An arrow!

There's another arrow!

FOLLOW THE ARROWS

<u>OWL</u> MY GOODNESS! IS THIS WHAT I THINK IT IS!?

Diary, we found one of Nellie Wingdale's TREASURE HUNT CLUES!!!

The arrows led deep into the forest.

It was so dark under all those trees, we hardly realized the sun was almost up!

We shouldn't tell anyone about the arrows yet since they might not lead to anything.

I agree. We need to find more clues before we say anything!

We climbed into our sleeping bags.

Imagine if we <u>do</u> find Nellie's treasure!

We could share it with everyone! That would be <u>flaptastic</u>!

Good day, Diary. Treasure hunters like us need all the sleep we can get!

♡ Follow the Clues! ♡

Wednesday

Tonight Mrs. Featherbottom surprised us with a cool activity: a forest obstacle course!

You and your project partner must work <u>together</u> to race through it.

30

She tied our wings together.

Ready, steady, go!

There were logs to crawl through,

stepping stones to jump across,

mud puddles to leap over,

and rope ladders to climb!

It was SO funny with our wings tied together! To be honest, I don't even know who won!

Afterward, while everyone else worked on their projects, Lucy and I went back to following arrows. We came out at a wide part of the river.

I don't see any more arrows. What do we do now?

Maybe this was all just someone's silly joke?

Wait, look at this!

Lucy found a clue carved into a rock:

The treasure you seek is on the other side.
But if you fly there, the clue will be denied.

So we have to cross the river.

But we're not allowed to fly . . .

There was no way for us to cross the river without flying.

We told them about Nellie's clues. And we showed them the message in the rock.

The treasure you seek is on the other side. But if you fly there, the clue will be denied.

Then we all agreed to start the Treasure Hunters Club!

We began to row across the river.

Just then, our oar hit a tree stump!

We found a clue!

Over the edge of the cliff,
though it's too heavy to lift,
is the next clue you can't miss.

We looked over the cliff's edge and saw a boulder with a rope tied around it.

This <u>must</u> be the next clue!

Argh! What if we fall?!

You <u>can</u> fly you know!

Oh, yeah.

We flew down to the boulder.

We tried and tried. But it was WAY too heavy to lift.

The sun was nearly up, so we rushed back to camp.

We'll try again tomorrow.

Don't tell anyone else about our hunt though. I can't wait to surprise them with Nellie's treasure!

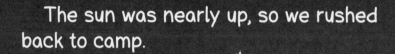

We all sat around the campfire.

My and George's catapult is <u>owlmazing</u>.

Good for you, Sue.

Have you and Lucy made <u>anything</u> for your project yet?

Um... we've sort of started on an umbrella.

Well, you'd better hurry. You're making it too easy for me to win that trophy!

Soon it was time to settle into our tents for the day. I felt bad for not telling Sue or any of the others about the treasure hunt.

I told Lucy how I was feeling.

Maybe we should tell them.

Let's just wait to see what we find tomorrow.

Yeah, we still might not even find anything!

Sue is right about our project though. We need to get to work!

When everyone else was asleep, we started weaving our umbrella. But we were too tired to get much work done.

Oh Diary, we'll never finish our project by Friday! But if we find the treasure, everyone will be _so_ happy, it won't matter. Right? On the other **WING**, what if we don't find the treasure?!

♥ Let's All Pulley Together! ♥

Thursday

Tonight Mrs. Featherbottom took us on a nature walk. It was so much fun that I stopped worrying about the project and the treasure!

We learned how to identify footprints.

We made bark rubbings.

We went on a bug hunt.

Zara drew a picture in the sand.

We found everything we needed. Then we got to work.

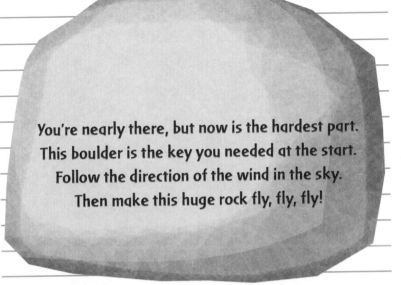

You're nearly there, but now is the hardest part.
This boulder is the key you needed at the start.
Follow the direction of the wind in the sky.
Then make this huge rock fly, fly, fly!

We brainstormed what to do next.

Well, we can find out which way the wind blows.

How?

We can make a wind sock.

Lucy told us how to build a wind sock.

It's working!
The wind blows that way because of the mountains behind us.
Now what do we do?
I have no idea.

The sun was almost up. We still hadn't found the treasure AND <u>none</u> of us had finished our forest projects. How will we get everything done before we head home tomorrow?!

We whispered to one another around the campfire.

What should we do about our projects?

I know! We'll wake up before everyone else and work then.

Good plan.

So we'll finish our projects first thing tomorrow. Yay!

♡ Find That Treasure! ♡

Friday

DISASTER!

All six of us overslept! We had no time to finish our projects!

We watched everyone else show what they'd made . . .

The stick flutes sounded **HOOTIFUL**.

The hammock looked super comfy.

Even Sue and George's catapult was **OWLSOME**.

Then it was time for me and Lucy to share what we had made.

It was time for us Treasure Hunters to share our secret.

The thing is . . .

None of us have finished our projects.

Because we've been busy —

Searching for Nellie's hidden treasure!

Then Sue laughed. HA HA!

There isn't REALLY any treasure!

I couldn't believe Sue was laughing. Nellie's treasure IS real, and our club is going to prove it.

We showed everyone the arrows and the clues we found using our raft, pulley, and wind sock.

You <u>did</u> find clues! And <u>you</u> built very USEFUL things. These <u>are</u> your projects!

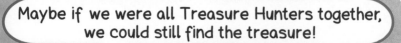

Maybe if we were all Treasure Hunters together, we could still find the treasure!

Now everyone was excited about the treasure hunt! (Except for Sue. She still thought it was silly.)

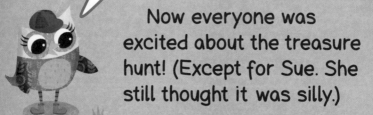

We read the last clue again.

You're nearly there, but now is the hardest part.
This boulder is the key you needed at the start.
Follow the direction of the wind in the sky.
Then make this huge rock fly, fly, fly!

You found the first clue over there.

That must be the <u>start</u>!

Aha! So we need to get the boulder over the river.

Yes! We need to <u>fly</u> it in the direction of the wind.

But how? It's so heavy!

We can't carry it.

We need something strong enough to <u>throw</u> it!

Then George whispered to me.

I think we might be able to help, but you'll have to ask Sue.

65

The boulder flew across the river!

It landed on one
end of a strange log.
A smaller rock on the
other end rocketed
off the log.

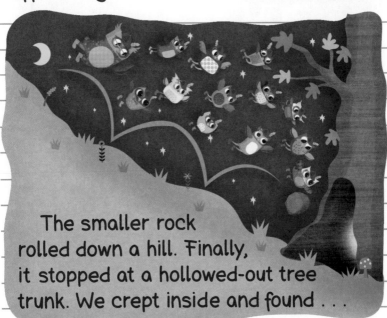

The smaller rock
rolled down a hill. Finally,
it stopped at a hollowed-out tree
trunk. We crept inside and found . . .

NELLIE'S TREASURE!

The treasure you seek was already found.
It is the friends who helped you,
The family who support you,
The smarts you used to get here,
And the gifts of the forest all around.

We thought about our friends and families, the amazing things we have made, and the forest fun we've had on this trip. We knew what to do.

Mrs. Featherbottom told us she was proud of us and of the useful projects we had built. She said we were all winners! She gave us trophies filled with candy coins – our very own treasure!

It's a Treasure Hunters Party!

Rebecca Elliott was a lot like Eva when she was younger: She loved making things and hanging out with her best friends. Now that Rebecca is older, not much has changed — except that her best friends are her husband, Matthew, and their children. She still loves making things, like stories, cakes, music, and paintings. But as much as she and Eva have in common, Rebecca cannot fly or turn her head all the way around. No matter how hard she tries.

Rebecca is the author of JUST BECAUSE and MR. SUPER POOPY PANTS. OWL DIARIES is her first early chapter book series.

OWL DIARIES

How much do you know about Eva's Campfire Adventure?

What do Eva and her classmates do to set up their campsite? Reread pages 14–15.

Do you know the tune of Eva's favorite campfire song? If not, try singing it using the name "Bingo" instead of "Baxter." Now do you know it?

The Treasure Hunters move a boulder using a pulley, which is a type of simple machine. Look at Zara's diagram on page 51. Explain how the pulley works.

When Eva goes on a nature walk, she forgets her worries. What are some ways you like to relax? Do you find nature calming?

Make a bark rubbing! Hold a thick piece of paper tightly up against a tree trunk. Then use pencils or crayons to rub the bark pattern onto your paper. Use different colors and trees to make a HOOTIFUL picture!

Camping with my friends was fun, Diary. But I am looking forward to seeing my family again. I've missed them so much!

Nellie Wingdale was right: There is no greater treasure than your friends and family.

See you next time, Diary.

We danced around the campfire, ate candies, and drank warm acorn syrup! At the end of the night, we flew home.